PARENTS AND CAREGIVERS,

Stone Arch Readers are designed to provide enjoyable reading experiences, as well as opportunities to develop vocabulary, literacy skills, and comprehension. Here are a few ways to support your beginning reader:

* Talk with your child about the ideas addressed in the story.

* Discuss each illustration, mentioning the characters, where they are, and what they are doing.

* Read with expression, pointing to each word. You may want to read the whole story through and then revisit parts of the story to ensure that the meanings of words or phrases are understood.

* Talk about why the character did what he or she did and what your child would do in that situation.

* Help your child connect with characters and events in the story.

Remember, reading with your child should be fun, not forced. Each moment spent reading with your child is a priceless investment in his or her literacy life.

GAIL SAUNDERS-SMITH, PH.D.

STONE ARCH **READERS**

are published by Stone Arch Books
A Capstone Imprint
151 Good Counsel Drive, P.O. Box 669, Mankato, Minnesota 56002
www.capstonepub.com

Library of Congress Cataloging-in-Publication data
is available on the Library of Congress website.

Library Binding: 978-1-4342-1872-8
Paperback: 978-1-4342-2307-4

Summary: Three Claws visits
Snorp in the city.

Creative Director: Heather Kindseth
Designer: Bob Lentz
Production Specialist: Michelle Biedscheid

Reading Consultants:
Gail Saunders-Smith, Ph.D.
Melinda Melton Crow, M.Ed.
Laurie K. Holland, Media Specialist

THREE CLAWS
IN THE CITY

BY CARI MEISTER

ILLUSTRATED BY
DENNIS MESSNER

STONE ARCH BOOKS
a capstone imprint

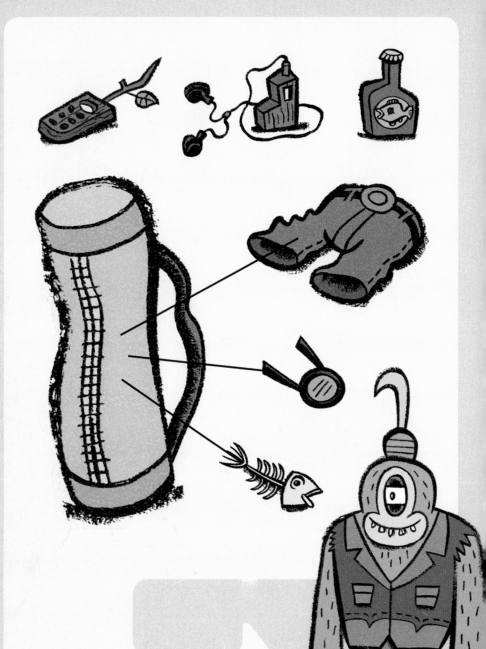

THREE CLAWS

This is Three Claws.

He lives on top of a mountain.

Three Claws has a big job.
He watches over the mountain.
If people come, Three Claws
scares them away.

Three Claws loves his job.
But it is hard work.

He runs a lot. He roars a lot.

His eye is always watching.

Three Claws needs a break.

"Go on a trip," say the other monsters.

"Good idea!" says Three Claws. "I will visit my friend Snorp in the city!"

Three Claws writes to Snorp.

This is Snorp. He lives in the busy city.

He reads the letter from Three
Claws.

"Oh no!" he yells.

Snorp loves Three Claws.
Three Claws is fun. Three Claws
is brave. Three Claws has great
ideas.

But when they are together,
Snorp always gets hurt.

One time, they went rock climbing. It started out fun. They were up so high! But Three Claws did not watch his step.

One time, the two friends went bungee jumping.

"You can use your tongue!" Three Claws had said.

That was a bad idea.

The last time Three Claws came to visit, they took a circus class.

Snorp only broke one leg
that time.

So Snorp writes back to
Three Claws.

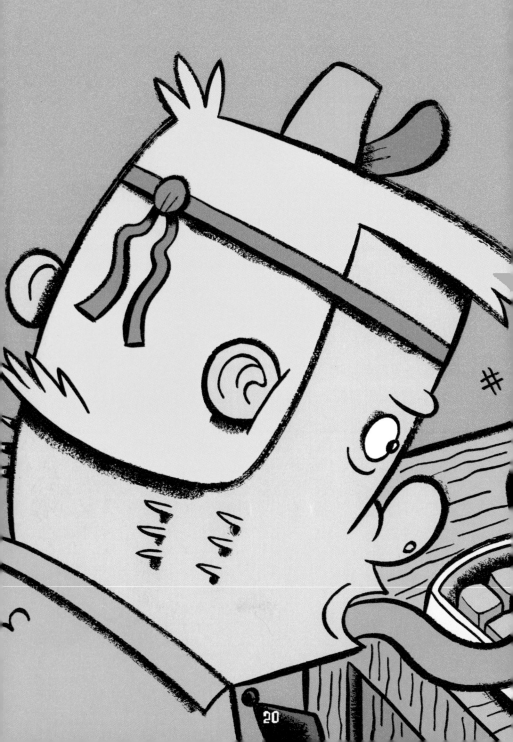

Dear Three Claws,
I got your letter. I would love to see you!
We can watch movies. We can play games.
No crazy sports! I don't want to get hurt.
See you on Sunday.
Your Friend,
Snorp

ps. I will get some rotten fish for you.
pps. I love your drawing.

On Sunday, Three Claws arrives.

The two friends play video games. They watch monster movies. It is a great day.

On Monday and Tuesday,
the two friends play more
video games. They watch more
monster movies.

On Wednesday, Three Claws
wants to do something new.

"This is my last day here,"
he says. "Let's go to the water
park."

Snorp is not sure. He does not
want to get hurt.

"Please!" begs Three Claws.

The water park is busy. Three
Claws points to the tallest slide.

"Let's go," he says.

"I will watch," says Snorp.
"Have fun!"

Three Claws climbs the ladder.

He slides. He spins. He splashes!

But wait! Three Claws cannot swim!

"Help! Help!" he screams.

Snorp runs. He jumps. He swims.

"Grab my tongue!" he says.

Hooray! Three Claws is saved!

The two friends spend the rest
of the day in the kiddy pool.
They have a great time!

And Snorp does not get hurt.
Well, not too much.

THE END

STORY WORDS

mountain	video
bungee	hooray
tongue	kiddy

Total Word Count: 365

READ MORE MONSTER STORIES!